POCKET HEROES

SHORT JOHN SILVER

DAVE WOODS
CHRIS INNS

ORCHARD

SHORT JOHN SILVER

For Fiona, Joe and Isabella, my not so scurvy crew
C.I.

For my daughter, Florence – whose birth helped Chris and I
breathe life into this series
D.W.

ORCHARD BOOKS
338 Euston Road, London NW1 3BH
Orchard Books Australia
Level 17/207 Kent Street, Sydney, NSW 2000

First published in 2013
First paperback publication in 2014

ISBN 978 1 40831 353 4 (hardback)
ISBN 978 1 40831 359 6 (paperback)

Text and illustrations © Dave Woods and Chris Inns 2013

A CIP catalogue record for this book is available
from the British Library.

1 3 5 7 9 10 8 6 4 2 (hardback)
1 3 5 7 9 10 8 6 4 2 (paperback)

Printed in Great Britain

Orchard Books is a division of Hachette Children's Books,
an Hachette UK company.

www.hachette.co.uk

Now, you may not know this, but long before Long John Silver was long – he was short. Very short.

In fact, he was Short John Silver!

One day, long ago, the place where all the scariest (and hairiest) pirates loved to go was a tavern called The Hook and Eyepatch.

All the most terrible pirates gathered there. Pirates like RedBeard, BlackBeard, BlueBeard and TartanBeard. And the stories they told were even more terrible than the pirates (who were very terrible indeed!).

On this day a new pirate showed up. Unlike the others, this pirate had no beard at all – not a single whisker.

It was Short John Silver!

"AHOY, UP THERE!" he cried.

All the pirates fell silent. Terribly silent.

"Who said that?" said BlueBeard.

The pirates looked around. They couldn't see anyone.

"Must've been the wind," said BlackBeard.

"Er, sorry about that," said RedBeard. "That'll be me – my bottom's all at sea!"

"HA-HAAR!" the pirates laughed.

(Terrible pirates love terrible jokes, too.)

"DOWN 'ERE, YOU BEARDED BARNACLES!" cried Short John Silver.

The big pirates peered down at the little pirate. Some with fierce eyes. Some with beady eyes. Some with just one eye.

"I be looking for Captain Poopdeck!" said Short John Silver. "They say 'e's the worst, most cursed pirate captain on the high seas."

There was a moment's silence, then...

"AYE, THAT BE TRUE!" said a terrible voice.

The pack of pirates parted.

There stood a truly terrible pirate.

Instead of a smile, he had a scowl.

Instead of a hand, he had a hook.

And instead of a parrot on his shoulder, he had a vulture.

"I BE CAPTAIN POOPDECK!" said Captain Poopdeck.

"With a name like that, you must be very terrible indeed," said Short John Silver.

The other pirates giggled.

But not for long.

Captain Poopdeck silenced them with a terrible glance.

"How'd you be getting a name like that, Cap'n?" asked Short John Silver.

"You've heard of a wooden leg?" said Captain Poopdeck.

"Aye."

"Well, my injury was a little higher."

"Where exactly?" asked Short John Silver.

"Put it this way, I've got a few nicknames," said Captain Poopdeck.

BARREL-BUM!

"Get the idea?" said the Captain.

"Aye, Cap'n Teak-cheeks!" said Short John Silver.

"That's enough cheek from you, shrimp."

"I'm no shrimp – I'm known as Short John Silver," said Short John Silver.

(Which was true, except that he wasn't actually known yet.)

"And what do ye want with terrible me?" continued Captain Poopdeck.

"Not just terrible you," said Short John Silver. "I need your terrible crew and your terrible ship, too!"

Captain Poopdeck growled. "Give me one good reason why we should help ye!"

"THIS IS WHY!" shouted Short John Silver, and whipped out his tiny cutlass!

The pirates gasped and took a step back.

Short John Silver pulled a scroll from his pocket…SWISH, his cutlass sliced the air…SNICK, the string was cut and…FLAP, the scroll rolled open…

"A TREASURE MAP!" roared the pirates.

The pirates jigged and yo-ho-hoed
and jumped for joy (except
those with peg legs – who
hopped for joy, instead).

Because the one thing pirates love –
even more than being bad…is treasure.

Smack bang in the middle of the map was a big cross. And, next to it, some mighty big talk:

Here lies the
BURIED TREASURE
FIND IT AND YOU WILL BE
MIGHTILY
REWARDED!

Short John Silver held the map out to Captain Poopdeck. "Take me to TREASURE ISLAND and I'll let you and your crew share the Buried Treasure!"

"COUNT ME IN!" boomed Captain
Poopdeck.

"A-haar!" said Short John Silver.

"A-haar!" agreed Captain Poopdeck.

"A-haar!" said Short
John Silver again.

(Pirates, eh?)

"Now, let's be meeting my terrible
crew..." smiled Short John Silver.

SHORT JOHN SILVER

"Here be the who's who of my pirate crew!"

CAPTAIN POOPDECK

"The captain's made so many sailors cry, he's turned the sea salty!"

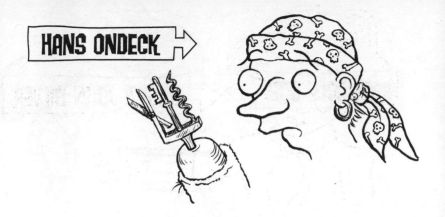

HANS ONDECK →

"Hans lost his hand in a pirate battle, but found a replacement... in a second-hand shop!"

SCURVY

"The only thing the cook's scared of is soap – he's never washed in his life!"

BARNACLE BOB

"The ship's carpenter loves sawing up planks – for people to walk off!"

FISHEYE LEN

"The only pirate lookout I've ever seen who has two eye patches!"

MIDSHIPMAN ROGER SCUTTLE

"He's been sunk so many times, 'is nickname is Johnny Dip!"

A-arrf!

PATCH

"The ship's dog – 'e loves chasin' catfish! A-harr!"

FISHBREATH

"Most ship's cats have four legs. This one has eight. Yep, it's an Octopuss!"

Short John Silver's crew gathered on the deck of the *Leaky Bucket*. Captain Poopdeck had been studying the treasure map for several minutes – but was looking confused.

Short John Silver reached up and turned the map the right way round.

"A-haar! That's better, m'lad!"

Suddenly the captain gasped. "Shiver me timbers!" (That's pirate speak for "I'm worried".)

"We've got to sail through... THE SEVEN SEAS!" cried Captain Poopdeck.

"That's why I need you, Cap'n," explained Short John Silver.

Captain Poopdeck shivered.

The crew shivered, too.

(Talk of THE SEVEN SEAS made even terrible pirates terribly scared.)

"THINK OF THE BURIED TREASURE!" Short John Silver reminded them.

"'E'S RIGHT!" bellowed Captain Poopdeck. "PREPARE TO WEIGH ANCHOR!"

"AYE-AYE, CAP'N!" cried the crew.

And so the *Leaky Bucket* set sail...

"Listen up, me hearties!" said Captain Poopdeck. "The first sea to navigate is THE SEA OF STORIES!"

"I LOVE FISHY TALES!" cried Short John Silver.

"STORY AHOY!" shouted Fisheye Len, the Lookout.

"Fish it out, Cap'n!" said Short John Silver.

"Grab me legs, shipmates!" cried Captain Poopdeck. The crew grabbed the captain and swung him down to the lapping waves. His hooked hand plunged into THE SEA OF STORIES and yanked out a book.

"*The Little Mermaid*!" cried Captain Poopdeck.

"It's only a tiddler," laughed Short John Silver. "Throw it back, I want a bigger one!"

"There she blows!" yelled the lookout.

A gigantic book surfaced beside the ship, its huge, white pages turning over in the waves.

"It's *Moby Dick*!" cried Short John Silver. "What a monster read!"

The great white tale jumped high out of the water and then landed, splashing Short John Silver with letters like W, E and T.

They sailed on, fishing out more tales.

"Throw back anything with a happy ending!" cried Short John Silver.

The pirates sniggered. (They hated happy endings.)

"Look, shipmates!" yelled Short John Silver. "We be leaving THE SEA OF STORIES."

"How do ye know?" cried the crew.

Short John Silver pointed at two words bobbing on the surface:

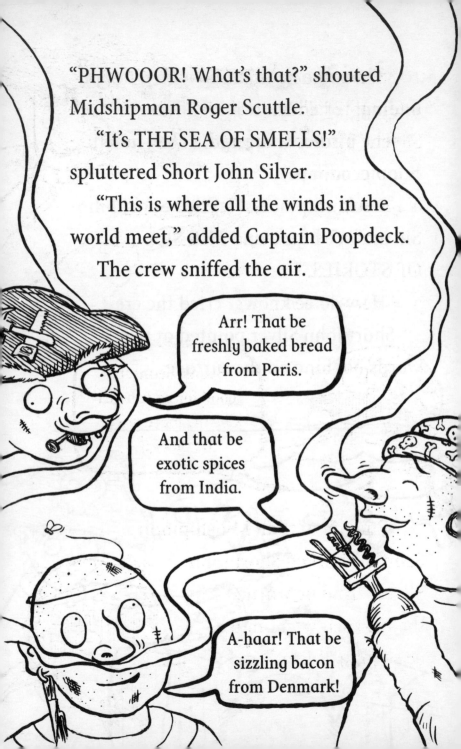

"PHWOOOR! What's that?" shouted Midshipman Roger Scuttle.

"It's THE SEA OF SMELLS!" spluttered Short John Silver.

"This is where all the winds in the world meet," added Captain Poopdeck. The crew sniffed the air.

Arr! That be freshly baked bread from Paris.

And that be exotic spices from India.

A-haar! That be sizzling bacon from Denmark!

"Sorry, me hearties!" interrupted Short John Silver. "That last draught be on account o' me eating too many beans for breakfast! Break out pegs for ye noses!"

Beans, beans, be good for your heart Cos the more ye eat, the more ye—

"Enough of that, Midshipman Scuttle!" barked Short John Silver. "And be warned – the next sea won't make ye so jolly, Roger."

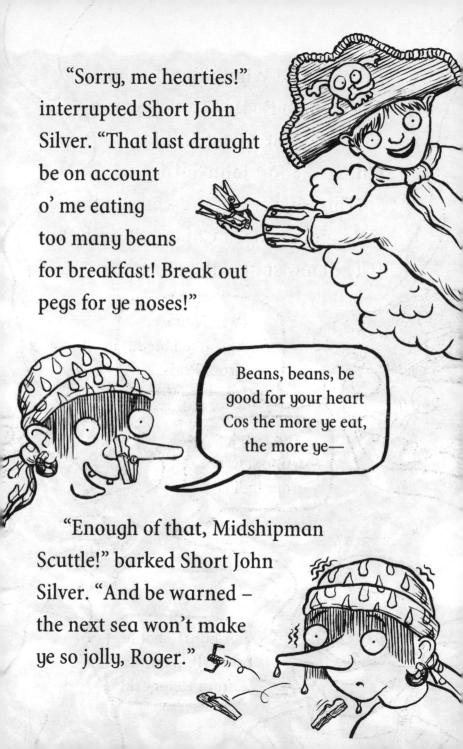

Short John Silver was right.
It was THE SEA OF SKELETONS!

He watched as the terrified
captain and his crew fled
below deck. They dived into
their cabins. They
locked their
doors.

They crawled under their bunks.
They closed their eyes.
And they thought of their mummies.
And how did they lock their doors?
   Yep, with Skeleton keys!

Up on deck, Short John Silver was playing with the only pirate who wasn't scared. It was Patch, the pirate dog! Short John Silver fished out a gigantic whalebone for him.

Patch the dog's tail was a-wag with excitement.

"Aye, Patch. This'll keep you happy for a long, long, long, long time!"

"The next sea be the most beautiful sea of all," smiled Short John Silver.

It was THE SEA OF COLOURS!

The rest of the pirates weren't convinced, though. Because (as we all know) a pirate's favourite colour – is black.

So the crew started telling jokes.

"What's WHITE on the outside, PINK in the middle, and swims?" asked Scurvy the Cook.

"A tuna sandwich!" giggled Short John Silver.

"What's YELLOW and bites?" asked Hans Ondeck.

"Shark-infested custard!" laughed the little pirate.

"Why did the lobster go RED?" asked
Barnacle Bob.

"Because the sea weed!" sniggered
Short John Silver.

(See, told you terrible pirates love
terrible jokcs.)

After a while, Captain Poopdeck
dipped a brush into THE SEA OF
COLOURS and painted Short John Silver.

"Ahoy there, Short John PURPLE!"
grinned the captain.

"Oh, no!" smiled Short John PURPLE.
"I'm MAROONED!"

The pirates laughed till they were
red, orange, yellow, green, blue, indigo
and violet in the face.

Next, the *Leaky Bucket* headed into…
THE SEA OF INVISIBILITY!

"I can't see the sea!" cried Fisheye
Len, the Lookout.

"How will I steer?" asked Captain
Poopdeck.

"Terribly!" said Short John Silver.

The pirates peeped over the ship's rail. It was a long, long way down. In fact, the ship felt so high, the crew got a fear of heights!

(A fancy word for this is vertigo – except when pirates get it, then it's called vertigo-ho-ho.)

"Look!" shouted Short John Silver, pointing to the seabed.

"SHIPWRECKS!" cried the pirates.

This made them even more nervous.

"What's wrong with the crew?" asked Captain Poopdeck.

"They're nervous wrecks," grinned Short John Silver.

Next came THE SEA OF SWEETS, which was (surprise, surprise) Short John Silver's favourite.

This sea was teeming with sweet life. Short John Silver peered overboard.

"Candy shrimps!" he cried to Scurvy the Cook. "Scoop me out a net full!"

But suddenly…

"LOOK OUT!" cried the lookout.

"Torpedoes on the starboard bow!"

BOOM! BOOM! BOOM! BOOM!

The ship's timbers shivered.

"We'll sink!" yelled Captain Poopdeck.

"No, we won't!" laughed Short John Silver. "They're liquorice torpedoes!"

After scoffing all the candy shrimps (and a whole shoal of fizzy fish), Short John Silver was nicely stuffed. But his bad pirate crew ate…and ate…and ate…until finally…they got sweet-sick.

You see, bad pirates love sweets – because they make their teeth bad, too.

The next sea soon wiped the sickly smile off Short John Silver's face.

It was…THE SEA OF STORMS!

"TIE YOURSELVES TO THE SHIP'S MAST!" yelled Short John Silver to the crew. "Or ye'll be washed overboard!"

"ME FIRST!" howled Scurvy the Cook. (The idea of being washed terrified him!)

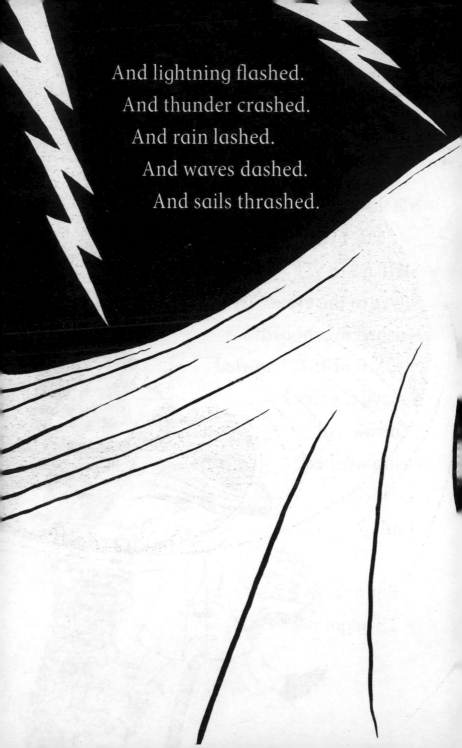

And lightning flashed.
And thunder crashed.
And rain lashed.
And waves dashed.
And sails thrashed.

But at last.
They got past.

"TREASURE ISLAND AHOY, SHORT JOHN SILVER!" shouted the lookout at last.

"Not long till we find THE BURIED TREASURE!" grinned Captain Poopdeck.

"Yes...er...A-haar," mumbled Short John Silver.

The eager pirates rushed ashore...

And noticed that things weren't quite how they should be.

For a start, they didn't need the treasure map, because everywhere they looked were signs saying:

and...

and even...

(Yes, the terrible crew
had a terrible surprise.)

"THE BURIED TREASURE'S JUST A PIRATE PUB!" roared Captain Poopdeck.

"WITH A RESTAURANT ATTACHED!" snarled Hans Ondeck.

"AND A KIDDIES' MENU!" growled Scurvy, the Cook.

Meanwhile, Short John Silver had gone (very) quiet.

"Forget the single cross, lads," said a fuming Captain Poopdeck, screwing up the treasure map. "WE'VE BEEN DOUBLE-CROSSED!"

The crew surrounded Short John Silver.

Captain Poopdeck smiled a crocodile smile. "It's time this pipsqueak of a pirate learnt to walk the plank…"

Suddenly, a big lady (with an even bigger grin) ran out of The Buried Treasure Inn.

"LITTLE JOHNNY!" she cried. "WHERE'VE YOU BEEN?"

She gave Short John Silver a mum-sized hug. (And hugs, as we all know, don't come any bigger than that.)

Then she smothered him with kisses.

"A-HUUUR-YUK!" shouted the horrified pirates, backing away. (Pirates hate kisses.)

Mmwaah! Mmwaah!

Short John Silver's mum turned to the crew. "You perfectly polite pirates!" she smiled. "You brought my darling Johnny back! The little rascal's always sneaking off on adventures. But somehow, he always manages to find his way home!"

"Yeah, thanks for the lift, shipmates!" winked Short John Silver, safely hidden behind his mother.

"GRRRRR!" growled the grumpy group.

Short John Silver's mum continued. "Now, as the landlady of The Buried Treasure, let me thank you all by treating you to a slap-up feast!"

As soon as the pirates heard the word 'feast', the angry grumblings turned to hungry rumblings – of their tummies!

And so the pirates got to enjoy THE BURIED TREASURE after all.

And what became of Short John Silver?
Well, that's another story…

DAVE WOODS
CHRIS INNS